"It isn't fair!" Charlie said, and he was right.

"Having no Halloween is the worst thing that could happen!" he said, but he was wrong.

There was one worse thing, and we heard about it in the morning announcements at school. . . .

Firegirl

Tony Abbott

SCHOLASTIC INC.
New York Toronto London Auckland
Sydney Mexico City New Delhi Hong Kong

ISBN 978-0-545-24390-2

16 15   13 14 15/0

Printed in the U.S.A.   40

First Scholastic printing, February 2010

The text was set in Aldus, and the display type is Merss ITC.

For her

Firegirl

Barbara Robinson

The ~~Worst~~ Best
Halloween
Ever

SCHOLASTIC INC.
New York Toronto London Auckland Sydney
Mexico City New Delhi Hong Kong Buenos Aires

ISBN-13: 978-0-545-13382-1
ISBN-10: 0-545-13382-3

12 11 10 9 8 7 6 5 4 3 2   8 9 10 11 12 13/0

Printed in the U.S.A.   40

First Scholastic printing, October 2008

Typography by Alicia Mikles

This book is for my best boys — my grandsons,
Tomas, Marcos, and Lucas

The ~~Worst~~ Best Halloween Ever

It was the principal's idea, but it was the Herdmans' fault, according to my mother.

"Don't blame Mr. Crabtree," she said. "It wasn't Mr. Crabtree who piled eight kids into the revolving door at the bank. It wasn't Mr. Crabtree who put the guppies on the pizza. It was one of the Herdmans, or some of the Herdmans, or all of the Herdmans . . . so if there's no Halloween this year, it's their fault!"

Of course the Herdmans couldn't cancel

Halloween everywhere. That's what I told my little brother, Charlie. Charlie kept saying, "I can't believe this!"—as if it was unusual for the Herdmans to mess things up for everybody else.

It wasn't unusual. There were six Herdmans—Ralph, Imogene, Leroy, Claude, Ollie, and Gladys—plus their crazy cat, which was missing one eye and half its tail and most of its fur and any good nature it ever had. It bit the mailman and it bit the Avon lady, and after that it had to be kept on a chain, which is what most people wanted to do with the Herdmans.

I used to wonder why their mother didn't do that with them, but, after all, there were six of them and only one of her. She didn't hang around the house much anyway, and you couldn't really blame her—even my mother said you couldn't really blame her.

They lived over a garage at the bottom of

Sproul Hill and their yard was full of whatever used to be in the garage—old tires and rusty tools and broken-down bicycles and the trunk of a car (no car, just the trunk)—and I guess the neighbors would have complained about the mess except that all the neighbors had moved somewhere else.

"Lucky for them!" Charlie grumbled. "They don't have to go to school with Leroy like I do."

Like we all do, actually. The Herdmans were spread out through Woodrow Wilson School, one to each grade, and I guess if there had been any more of them they would have wiped out the school and everybody in it.

As it was they'd wiped out Flag Day when they stole the flag, and Arbor Day when they stole the tree. They had ruined fire drills and school assemblies and PTA bake sales, and they let all the kindergarten mice out of their cage and then filled up the cage with guinea pigs.

The whole kindergarten got hysterical about this. Some kids thought the guinea pigs ate their mice. Some kids thought the guinea pigs *were* their mice, grown gigantic overnight. They were all scared and sobbing and hiccuping, and the janitor had to come and remove the guinea pigs.

All the mice got away, so I guess if you were a mouse you would be crazy about the Herdmans. I don't know whether mice get together and one of them says, "How was your day?"—but if that happens, these mice would say, "Terrific!"

"So was that it, Beth?" Charlie asked me. "The mice and the guinea pigs? Was that, like, the last straw, and then everybody said, 'All right, that's it, the last straw . . . no Halloween'? Was that it?"

"I don't think so," I said. "I think it was everything else."

There had been a lot of everything else

because Labor Day was late, so school started late. Parents had an extra week to buy their kids school shoes and get their hair cut; kids had an extra week to finish the fort or tree house or bike trail or whatever else they'd been building since June; and teachers had an extra week to pray they wouldn't have any Herdmans, I guess. . . . And of course the Herdmans had an extra week, too, to tear up whatever they'd missed during the summer.

That turned out to be a lot and, as usual with the Herdmans, it wasn't always things you would *expect* them to do.

The police guard at the bank said that he had seen them come in. "Can't miss *them*!" he said. "So I went right over and stood by the big fish tank. I figure, if I see a bank robber coming I'll defend the money, but if I see those kids coming I'll defend the fish." He shook his head and sighed. "Didn't occur to me to hang around the revolving door."

Nobody got hurt and everybody got out all right, but they had to call the fire department to take the door apart, and they had to close the bank till they got the door back up.

The fire chief said he never saw anything like it. "Two kids," he said, "maybe even three kids might go in that door at the same time to see what would happen, but this was eight kids! What you had was one section of a revolving door full of kids. Couldn't move the door forward, couldn't move it back, had to take it down . . . unless, well, you couldn't just leave them in there."

This was supposed to be a joke, but most people thought it would have been a great opportunity to shut the Herdmans up *somewhere*, even in a revolving door.

It *would* have been a great opportunity, except that by then it wasn't Herdmans in the door. It was eight different kids, including Charlie.

"Why?" my father asked him. "Why would you follow the Herdmans anywhere, let alone into a revolving door?"

Charlie shrugged and looked up at the ceiling and down at the floor and finally said he didn't know. "It was just that they were all around," he went on. "There were Herdmans in front of us and Herdmans in back of us, and then Ralph said, 'Let's see how many kids will fit in the door,' and so . . . " He shrugged again.

The bank manager was mad because of his door, and the bank guard was mad because he picked the wrong thing to guard, but nobody blamed him. How could he know what the Herdmans were going to do? Most of the time, I don't think even the Herdmans knew what they were going to do.

I don't think they *planned* to mix up the mice and the guinea pigs until they happened to see some guinea pigs, and I don't think they decided to find some kids and shove them into a revolving door until they happened to see the door and a bunch of kids all at the same place at the same time.

There probably wouldn't have been any trouble at the pizza parlor either if Mr. Santoro hadn't introduced a new variety— sardine pizza—and *that* wouldn't have caused any trouble if Boomer Malone didn't have to get rid of his guppies.

Boomer started out with two guppies in a fishbowl, and by the next week he had about a hundred guppies in jars and bottles and bowls. Mrs. Malone told my mother that she even found guppies in ice cube trays.

Boomer's original idea had been to sell the guppies, but he finally had to pay Leroy Herdman fifty cents to take them away. According to Gladys, they were going to dump all the guppies into their bathtub and then charge kids a quarter to come and see the guppies go down the drain, all at once.

"It won't hurt them," Gladys said. "They'll just go wherever the water goes and swim around. They'll like it."

Maybe so, but it never happened. Before they got the guppies home to the bathtub, Leroy and Claude and Gladys stopped in the pizza parlor, saw six sardine pizzas on the counter, and immediately swapped guppies for the sardines.

Nobody ever did think that sardine pizza would be a success but, as Mr. Santoro said, "After *that*, sardine pizza didn't have a chance."

The customers agreed. One man said he didn't think he'd ever eat *any* kind of pizza again. "Wasn't looking," he said, " . . . took a bite, and the next thing I knew there was half a guppie in my mustache."

So there really wasn't any last straw, but by the time school finally started, so many people were so mad at the Herdmans for so many reasons that you knew something was going to happen.

"It's got to stop!" the mayor said . . . but nobody knew that "it" was going to be Halloween.

2

It was only natural for people to blame our principal, because Mr. Crabtree didn't like Halloween in the first place. He didn't want anyone to wear costumes to school or put up Halloween decorations or have homeroom parties, and every year he sent home a note that said Halloween would not be an acceptable excuse for tardiness or late homework or headaches or stomachaches or failure to stay awake in class or anything else.

One year Eugene Preston went trick-or-treating without a flashlight, fell over the Johannesons' birdbath, and broke his ankle, and Eugene was scared to come to school.

He even had a dream about it. "Mr. Crabtree took away my crutch," he said, "and he made me hop everywhere—up and down the stairs and outdoors for recess—and he made me play basketball. In my dream I kept telling him that I had a broken ankle, and he just kept hollering, 'No excuse! No excuse!'"

"Well, that's just silly," my mother said when Charlie told her about Eugene's dream. "Mr. Crabtree didn't say anything about broken bones. He was just saying don't stay up past your bedtime and don't forget your schoolwork and don't eat a lot of candy and get sick. What's wrong with that?"

Nothing, if you were a mother . . . but these were the exact things that Charlie and I expected to do on Halloween. Actually, these were the exact things we *did* do on

Halloween, except for eating too much candy. We never ended up with too much candy and neither did anyone else, thanks to the Herdmans.

They were around every corner and behind every tree on Halloween. They didn't dress up—they didn't have to, because they looked like Halloween all the time. Sometimes kids even dressed up like them. They didn't go trick-or-treating—but they didn't have to do that either as long as everyone else did, collecting candy and gum and money for the Herdmans to take away from them.

Of course this meant that they had more time than the rest of us. They didn't have to pick out or invent costumes, try them on, and cut holes to see out of. They didn't have to be polite to the neighbors and say thank you and only take one trick-or-treat candy. They didn't have to stay on their own block and come in at 8:30 . . . so they were free to run all over town, starting fires and breaking windows and moving street signs and stealing anything that wasn't nailed down.

Although they had done all these things at one time or another, they had never done all of them at once, which was about the only good thing you could say for them.

"Well, at least they didn't set fire to the hospital," people would say if they set fire to something else, and when they ran off with the Rotary Club cake (it had "Rotary Club—Happy Halloween!" spelled out in M&M's, and it was supposed to serve eighty-five people so I don't know what they ate instead), everybody said "Well, at least it was a cake they stole. It wasn't somebody's life savings."

Last year they jimmied open the cages at the Animal Rescue and let all the dogs and cats out. The dogs and cats didn't know it was Halloween, or why everybody had on sheets and rubber noses and aluminum foil underwear . . . and kids didn't know where all the dogs and cats came from, so there was a lot of barking and yelling and crying.

Naturally there were parents trying to find their kids and police trying to get things under control, and the dog officer trying to collect whatever animals he could get hold of, along with the Fire Rescue truck and paramedics with dog-bite medicine.

There wasn't anything for the paramedics to do because nobody got bitten and nobody got scratched, but they did have to rescue Alice Wendleken.

Like everything else in Alice's life, her Halloween costume always had to be better than everyone else's—more original and unusual, or more beautiful and sparkly. When Alice said "Trick or treat!" she wanted people to gasp at the wonder of her, and maybe applaud.

That year she was a hot dog, with the bun and the mustard and all. At the last minute she thought it would be more realistic if she smelled like a hot dog, so she cut one up into little pieces and glued them inside the bun part of her costume.

It was realistic all right. Once the dogs got a whiff of Alice they thought she was lunch, and they all joined in, snuffling and sniffing and licking her.

Somebody called Mrs. Wendleken, but by the time she got there the police had Alice out of her costume, wrapped up in a blanket, and sitting in the police car. Mrs. Wendleken didn't see that—what she saw was the remains of the costume, mostly the mustard part and pieces of the bun, and a lot of dogs sitting around licking their chops.

Mrs. Wendleken said later that of course she knew the dogs hadn't eaten Alice up, leaving nothing but pieces of mustard and hot dog bun. "But think how it looked!" she said. "Naturally I got a little excited."

My mother said hysterical was more like it, " . . . wanting all those dogs locked up for observation, in case they were mad instead of just bewildered!"

"Don't forget the Herdmans," I said. "She wanted them locked up, too."

Of course none of that happened, so Mrs. Wendleken was furious. She stayed furious, too, and when she heard about the guppies and the revolving door, she said it was obvious that the Herdmans were out of control and there was no telling what they would do this year on Halloween.

She wasn't the only one.

The police chief said the Herdmans and Halloween together always gave him nightmares, and this year looked like it could be the worst one yet.

Then the fire chief chimed in. "Do you

know what happens to other fire departments on Halloween?" he said. "Other fire
departments get false alarms . . . a lot of false
alarms. I'd love to get false alarms on
Halloween! What I get is little Herdman
fires." It was true, he said, that the
Herdmans never seemed to set fire to anything important, " . . . but I can't count on
that. This could be the year they happen to
burn down the First National Bank."

The druggist said he was going to board
up his windows, and Mr. Kline at the hardware store said he was going to sleep in the
back room, just in case. And the next thing
we knew, the mayor said, "This has got to
stop!" . . . and he *did* mean Halloween.

He announced it at the Rotary meeting—
"No Halloween"; and he announced it at the
town council meeting—"No Halloween";
and then it was in the newspaper, on the front
page—"MAYOR CANCELS HALLOWEEN."

. . . out of concern for public safety, the arti-
cle said, *and to avoid possible damage to prop-
erty. Local merchants will neither purchase nor
stock the usual supply of Halloween candy.*

So that was it . . . no Halloween, no
candy.

Charlie said he was going to have
Halloween anyway. He said he was going to
put on a costume and go trick-or-treating and
everything, but he really wasn't. Neither was
I. Nobody was, because we couldn't have
Halloween all by ourselves.

You have to have kids on one end of
Halloween, to look forward to it and get
scary books out of the library and cut up
pumpkins and get dressed up and then, as
soon as it's dark, go trick-or-treating with
your friends.

Then you have to have grown-ups on the
other end of Halloween, to give you the old
sheets and pad you with pillows and fasten

you together with safety pins and hang around the house to hand out candy and, of course, supply the candy.

"It isn't fair!" Charlie said, and he was right.

"Having no Halloween is the worst thing that could happen!" he said, but he was wrong.

There was one worse thing, and we heard about it in the morning announcements at school.

3

The morning announcements are pretty boring, but you can usually find something else to think about. While Mr. Crabtree drones on about bus schedules and PTA notices, you can think about lunch or your science project or why Boomer Malone's retainer looks like Dracula fangs.

But that day there was big news.

"I'm sure you're all aware," Mr. Crabtree said, "that there will be no Halloween activities in our town this year . . . specifically, there will be no trick or treat. There will be no candy handouts—in fact, no candy at all."

There was one loud groan all over the school and a babble of complaints, but Mr. Crabtree ignored it. "This is owing," he went on, "to widespread misconduct by, I'm sorry to say, some of our Woodrow Wilson students."

"He means the Herdmans," Alice Wendleken hissed, as if everybody didn't already know that. Then Alice turned around and glared at Imogene Herdman, which Alice would never do if she wasn't four rows and seven seats away.

"No Halloween!" Imogene yelled, so I guess the Herdmans didn't read the newspaper. "Who says?"

Mr. Crabtree was still talking, so Mrs. Hazelwood said, "Sh-h, Imogene . . . the mayor says . . . now sh-h-h."

"The mayor and who else?" Imogene

looked at the PA speaker. "Him?"

"Everybody else," Alice said, "and it's your fault. You and Leroy and Gladys and Claude and all of you and your misconduct!"

I thought Alice was being too brave for her own good—now she would have to stay after school and clean the blackboard or dust erasers or mop the floor or write half a book or something till the coast was clear of Herdmans.

But maybe not, because Imogene didn't lunge across four rows and seven seats and smack Alice flat, right on the spot. She didn't even look mad. She looked really pleased with herself, as if misconduct was a hobby and the Herdmans were very good at it . . . which they were.

" . . . have never encouraged these activities in the past," Mr. Crabtree was saying. "However, this year . . . " The PA system crackled and hummed and quit and came back on, which is normal for it to do. " . . . going to have Halloween right here at Woodrow Wilson School on October twenty-ninth, and . . . " There were more crackles, as if somebody turned the microphone upside down, and you could hear voices all over the school . . . "got it wrong . . . date . . . wrong? . . . that's the wrong date!"

This was the first clue to what was going to happen to us. Mr. Crabtree didn't even know when Halloween *was*.

It was hard to believe. "How could he not know?" Stewart Walker said. "Unless he's so old that they didn't even have Halloween when he was a kid."

"I don't think he ever *was* a kid," Louella McCluskey said, and you could almost believe this. Of course Mr. Crabtree had to start out like everybody else, as a baby, but after that, once he got up on his feet, he was probably just like a small principal right from the beginning.

Nobody could figure out why Mr. Crabtree, of all people, would suddenly think Halloween was great and we should celebrate it.

"Why don't you just ask him?" Mrs. Hazelwood said, and then, "I'll make that an assignment—interview Mr. Crabtree for extra credit."

This is how teachers' minds work. They see extra credit in everything. Danny Filus once had to eat frogs legs in a restaurant, and Mrs. Hazelwood made him describe that for extra credit. Danny did a good job—only two kids got sick to their stomachs, but they were kids with pet frogs, so you could understand that.

"Volunteers, please, to interview Mr. Crabtree?"

No volunteers . . . except, of course, Alice Wendleken, who must have "I volunteer" tattooed on her chest.

"Thank you, Alice," Mrs. Hazelwood said, moving right along, "but I think . . . Stewart Walker might like the chance to earn some extra credit."

That was the last thing Stewart wanted to do, so he was practically under his desk, pretending to hunt for something on the floor, but it didn't do him any good. Mrs. Hazelwood can see around corners and through walls when she's on the trail of an extra credit.

I guess Stewart *tried* to interview Mr. Crabtree, but he probably didn't try very hard, and after a couple of days it didn't matter. After a couple of days everybody knew what Mr. Crabtree suddenly saw in Halloween.

Homework!

In every class, on every blackboard, there were special assignments and papers to write and things to look up: *Discuss Halloween cos-tumes—at least three paragraphs; Owls, bats, toads—choose one and discuss importance to Halloween in three paragraphs; Witch and broomstick. Why?—at least three paragraphs.*

"I have to read all about pumpkins," Charlie grumbled, "and then tell what all we do with them, and why."

"Pumpkin pie," I said. "You could write out the recipe for pumpkin pie." I thought that could be part of Charlie's paper, but he thought it could be the whole thing, so he was excited.

"You buy a can of pumpkin," Mother told him, "and you buy a pie shell. Put the pumpkin into the pie shell, put it into the oven, and bake it for forty-five minutes."

Charlie frowned. "Is that a recipe?"

"It's my recipe," Mother said.

Charlie's teacher said it was her recipe, too, but it better not be Charlie's paper or he would have to do it over. Kindergarten kids were lucky because they could just draw black cats and spooky houses the way they always did, and everyone in my class was lucky because Mrs. Hazelwood made all the assignments extra credit so you didn't *have* to do them.

"But of course," she said, "I hope all of you will take this opportunity to learn a little more about Halloween customs and traditions."

Right away Alice sharpened up her pencil and copied everything off the board, so you knew where all the extra credit was going to go.

"I don't care if she has all the extra credit in the world," Louella McCluskey said, "and I don't care about all the homework either, if it means we get to have Halloween after all. What are you going to be?" She sighed. "I guess I'll have to be a Pilgrim again."

Mrs. McCluskey had won a Pilgrim costume in a Chamber of Commerce Turkey Raffle and she didn't know what else to do with it, so Louella had already been a Pilgrim twice.

"Unless you want to trade," she said, "and be the Pilgrim this year. My mother won't let the costume go to waste."

"No," I said. "I'm going to be a belly dancer. I've got all the stuff for it—part of a sparkly bathing suit and some curtains and some long beads."

"Your mother won't let you be a belly dancer," Louella said, "with your whole middle showing and a jewel in your belly button!"

She was partly right. Mother said I absolutely could not have any jewel in my belly button. " . . . or anything else. And you can't go barefoot. You'll have to wear some kind of shoes."

"And if it's cold," I said, "I'll take that big lacy tablecloth for a shawl."

She looked surprised. "Well, it won't be cold in the school."

"But before that," I said, "when we go trick-or-treating."

"Beth, *nobody* is going to go trick-or-treating. You know that. It's the whole point of having Halloween at school."

Charlie yelped. "The whole point of Halloween *is* trick-or-treating for candy!"

"No, around here the whole point of Halloween is to beware of the Herdmans. Think about it—the dogs and cats and the Rotary Club cake . . . and you, Charlie, spray-painted green from head to foot!"

Of course Charlie wasn't the only spray-painted kid that year, and green wasn't the only color. There were red kids and blue kids and some gold kids, including Alice. Mrs. Wendleken said it was a miracle that Alice didn't die of clogged-up skin pores, but you could tell that Alice didn't really mind because she was still a little sparkly, here and there, two weeks after Halloween.

By now Mother was all warmed up to the subject. " . . . and the turkey farm," she went on, "when they turned on the sprinklers and nearly drowned all the turkeys. Yes, and the candy. Every year we buy all this candy and hand it out, and the Herdmans end up with all of it. I don't know what they do with all that candy, year after year. They couldn't possibly eat it."

I knew Charlie didn't want to talk about that, because one year Leroy Herdman made a bunch of kids, including Charlie, buy back their own candy.

"So," Mother said, "this year will be different. This year Halloween will be entirely in Woodrow Wilson School, controlled and safe. Don't forget—there almost wasn't any Halloween at all, because of the Herdmans. The mayor wasn't kidding when he called it off."

Charlie was still in shock about no trick or treat when Mother answered my main question. "I guess the Herdmans will be there," she said. "Can't very well keep them out, but nobody has to worry about them. After all, how much trouble can they cause right there in school, with teachers and parents everywhere? What can they do?" Mother smiled at us, as if that was that.

It wasn't.

4

Normally none of the Herdmans ever looked at the blackboard, or knew what was on it—especially if it was homework, which they never did anyway. So it was possible (this was Charlie's idea) that they wouldn't know about Halloween being at school and nowhere else.

"They'll go out," he said, "just the way they always do, looking for kids they can shove around and candy they can steal, and there won't be any! No kids, no candy! They won't know what happened. They'll go crazy!"

This made a great picture—all the Herdmans running up and down the empty streets, getting more and more frustrated, bumping into each other, maybe even running into trees or parked cars—but you knew it would never happen.

Besides, the Herdmans didn't have to read the blackboard to know all about the Woodrow Wilson Halloween. There were signs about it everywhere; all the first-graders had take-home notes pinned to them that said, *There will be no community Halloween. Come with your family to Woodrow Wilson School, 7 o'clock, Halloween night*; and almost every day Alice showed up with a new extra credit report about owls or bats or bonfires till Mrs. Hazelwood took pity on us ("Took pity on *herself*!" my mother said) and shut Alice down. "New school policy," Mrs. Hazelwood said. "No more extra credit."

Somebody had straightened Mr. Crabtree out about when Halloween really was, and every morning he got on the PA system to tell us what we had to look forward to on October 31—costume parade and prizes, cookie-decorating contest and prizes, Meet the Monsters . . .

"Meet the Monsters might be okay," I said.

"Not really," Stewart Walker said.

"It's better than drawing faces on cookies," I said.

"Not really. They aren't real monsters."

I stared at him. "Come on, Stewart! I know that."

He shook his head. "No, I mean they aren't normal monsters. These monsters are going to be parents. Yours . . . mine . . . " He pointed around the room. "His . . . hers . . . "

Parents? "Mine?" I asked.

"Well . . . mine. My father's going to be

Dracula. He's got these fake teeth, like Boomer's braces." He sighed.

"I'm sorry, Stewart," I said.

I didn't think my father would agree to be a monster, but Charlie wasn't so sure.

"Maybe not a monster," he said, "but there's other things people have to be— ghosts and ghouls and living dead and all."

"Ghouls?" my father said. "Living dead? I don't think so."

"Stewart Walker's father gets to be Dracula," Charlie said, "and Gloria Coburn's mother is a witch, and Margaret—"

"Well, good for them!" Mother said. "I told Hazel Wilson I wouldn't be anything like that, so they put me on the pumpkin committee. I really want to do my share because I want this to succeed. Just think . . . peaceful Halloweens, year after year! I guess I could be a witch if that's what they need . . . not one of the main ones, though."

"You'd be good on the pumpkin committee," I said. I didn't know what the pumpkin committee was, but it had to be better than your mother running around in witch clothes where everybody could see her.

I didn't know who the main witches were, but Alice did.

"There are three main witches," she told me. As usual, Mrs. Wendleken was in charge of everything so, as usual, Alice knew everything there was to know.

"There's the witch in charge of the boiling cauldron, and the witch in charge of the Mystery Swamp . . . "

"What's the Mystery Swamp?" I asked.

"I think it's going to be the fourth-grade room." Alice was so full of privileged information that all you had to do was ask What? or Why? or Who? and you would get the whole story.

"It was supposed to be the teachers' room,

but there's a big hole in the floor of the teachers' room. They keep a bookcase over it, but, naturally, there wouldn't be a bookcase in a swamp so they'd have to move it, and then somebody might fall down the hole. So it will probably be the fourth-grade room unless they use that for the monsters. . . . "

There was only one way to shut Alice up, or at least to get her to change the subject. "What are you going to be for Halloween?" I asked.

She looked around, very cautious. "If I say, will you not tell anybody? Swear?"

"Sure," I said. "Spit and swear."

"O-o-oh." Alice made a face. "Just swear," she said. "Spitting is dirty."

I guess it is, but if I want someone to keep an absolute secret, we'll spit and swear. In this case, though, it didn't matter because nobody was all that crazy to hear about Alice's Halloween costume.

"I'm going to be a Christmas tree," she said. "I'm going to be a lighted Christmas tree . . . and if anyone else is a lighted Christmas tree, I'll know you told!"

I didn't expect to hear about any Christmas tree costumes, lighted or not, but I didn't hear that much about any costumes. Usually that's *all* you hear about for the whole month of October—"What are you going to be for Halloween?"—and, except for Alice, people tell you.

They're going to buy their costume and be Superman or Batman or Wonder Woman . . . or they're going to make their costume and be an accident victim or a deck of cards or a two-hundred-year-old man or woman.

But this year—none of these.

"What are you going to be for Halloween?" I asked Boomer Malone. One year Boomer built himself a dinosaur costume out of sandpaper, so he had a lot to live up to.

"I don't know," he said. "I was going to wear my grandmother's old fur coat and be King Kong, but I don't want to do that after all." He shrugged. "I mean, with Halloween here at school . . . Maybe I'll just be a Happy Hobo."

The Happy Hobo was on a sign at the hardware store—"Happy Hobo Uses McAllister's Machine Oil" the sign says, and there's a picture of a smiling man in droopy jeans. Usually one or two people will be a Happy Hobo for Halloween, but I never expected Boomer to be one of them.

Charlie, too. "Maybe I'll be a Happy Hobo this year," he said.

"Well, that's not very interesting," Mother said. "Let's see if we can't think of something more exciting for you to be."

Normally my mother would be crazy about a Happy Hobo costume because it was so easy. "Oh, be a hobo," she would say. "All you need are your father's wash-the-car pants and a lot of dirt."

Now she was saying, "What about those old slipcovers in the attic . . . could you be something in slipcovers?"

"What did she mean?" Charlie asked me later. "Does she want me to be, like, a sofa or something?"

Mostly, I think, Mother just wanted us to be more excited about the Woodrow Wilson Halloween, because nobody was.

I knew, so far, of eleven Happy Hobos, not counting Boomer and Charlie, so that tells you something. This Halloween was going to be exactly what my mother said it would be—safe and controlled (by Mr. Crabtree and Mrs. Wendleken and the PTA) and peaceful and boring.

The only scary thing was going to be Mr. Walker's Dracula teeth.

5

The Herdmans must have figured that out because, according to Charlie, "They aren't going to come!"

"We're not going to waste our time on some dumb Woodrow Wilson PTA Halloween party with schoolteacher ghosts and no trick or treat" was what Ralph said.

"You have to go to it," Charlie told him. "I have to go. Everybody has to go. It's like a big school event."

As usual, there was more than one

Herdman on hand to comment about this. "A big school event would be that the school burned down," Claude said.

"Yeh!" Ollie grinned—the Herdman grin, sly and sneaky. "Or blew up."

You had to think twice about that because the Herdmans were famous for starting fires and blowing up garbage cans. Still, all they had to work with was a Junior Science kit that they stole from the hardware store, so the school was probably safe.

Of course anything the Herdmans stayed away from was sure to be popular with everybody else, so right away kids quit complaining about Mr. Crabtree and the homework and the family monsters. Nobody said they were glad about no trick-or-treating because nobody *was* glad about that.

"It's like we made a trade," Boomer Malone said. "We get rid of the Herdmans but we give up trick-or-treating."

It would be great if we could get rid of the Herdmans forever but that wasn't going to happen, so this was better than nothing.

"This is a *lot* better than nothing," my mother said. "Do you realize that this will be the first time in history that a Woodrow Wilson School event will go the way it's supposed to? Nothing will be stolen or blown up or burned down . . . or buried or dug up or"—she looked at Charlie—"wallpapered."

When Charlie was in the second grade, his teacher, Miss Evans, gave them some rolls of wallpaper to decorate their room for Parents' Night, and while the rest of the kids wallpapered their books and their lunchboxes and the blackboard, Leroy Herdman wallpapered Charlie to the coatroom door.

Miss Evans told my mother that she walked past him twice before it occurred to her that the door looked very strange.

"It was all . . . bumpy," she said. "But, my

goodness, I didn't think . . . well, you don't expect to find a child underneath the wallpaper. What alerted me the third time I went past that door was that the whole thing was moving. It looked like two or three puppies under a blanket, you know?"

Charlie had wallpaper paste all over himself—his clothes, his hair and eyebrows, in his ears and up his nose.

"Leroy's idea?" my mother said.

Charlie nodded. "I was supposed to jump out during Parents' Night and go 'Ta-da!' Leroy said it would be a big hit."

"Then why didn't Leroy do it?" Mother asked, scrubbing away at the wallpaper paste.

"He couldn't. He's allergic to wallpaper."

Mother never forgot this episode, and she never let Charlie forget it either, up to and including now. "Allergic to wallpaper!" she said.

"I was in the second grade!" Charlie

protested. "I didn't know any better then!"

I wasn't sure he knew any better now, so it was good that the Herdmans almost never did the same thing twice. Once they had wall-papered you, you could be pretty sure they wouldn't wallpaper you again. You could relax.

And if Charlie was right, and the Herdmans stayed away on Halloween, *every-one* could relax.

"I just wish I could be sure," Louella McCluskey said. "If I bring my little brother, Howard, to school that night and take him around to some of the things that aren't very scary, my mother will pay me eight dollars. But that's only if the Herdmans don't come. If they come my mother won't let me bring Howard. *I* still have to come." She sighed. "But I can't bring Howard."

"Why don't you ask Imogene?" I said. But we both knew that wouldn't help because she might say yes and it would be a lie, or she might say no and *that* would be a lie.

"I could ask her what she's going to be for Halloween," Louella said. "That might give me a clue."

It did.

"What am I going to be for Halloween?" Imogene said. "Well, I'm not going to be hanging around here in some secondhand bathrobe with a lot of fake witches and spooky music on the PA and little kid games like that . . . " She pointed to the second-grade room, where two PTA mothers were deciding where to hang up a sign that said "Pin the Tail on the Black Cat."

That satisfied Louella. "I know exactly what I'm going to do with my eight dollars," she said. "After Halloween they'll mark down the price on all the leftover Halloween costumes, and I'll buy one. I don't even care what it is, just so it's not a Pilgrim."

Louella was lucky, I thought, because this year the stores were full of Halloween costumes instead of Halloween candy.

"What did you expect?" Mother said, when Charlie came home moaning and groaning about the empty shelves at the supermarket. Charlie spends most of October checking out all the different candy, deciding what he wants most and what he doesn't want, and what he wants my mother to buy in case there's some left over. You'd think he never *saw* candy except at Halloween.

That's what Mother said. "You'd think you never *saw* candy except at Halloween, but you have candy all the time. I buy candy bars for the high school band trip every year. Your father buys me candy on my birthday. Aunt Elizabeth makes that wonderful fudge at Christmas."

"But that's not like Halloween candy,"

Charlie said. "Halloween candy is like . . . it's like . . . "

I helped him out. "It's like you get to have all the candy there is, all at once. You get to look at it, and count it, and separate it into little piles . . . "

"And trade it," Charlie said, "and eat it . . . "

"And hand it all over to the Herdmans," Mother said. "Don't forget that part."

But what Charlie couldn't forget was the empty shelves at the supermarket. "There isn't *anything* there," he kept saying. "No candy at all, not even healthy candy like PowerBars."

Mother said there was no such thing as healthy candy, and I guess she was getting tired of this subject, because she changed it. "Just wait till you get to school on Halloween night," she said, " . . . lots of surprises!"

What surprises? I wondered. We already

knew about the Mystery Swamp and the boiling cauldron and the monsters, and anything we didn't know about Alice would be glad to tell us—unless my mother had some private surprise. Did they talk her into being a witch? Or some other gross thing?

As far as I knew she was still on the pumpkin committee, and there were notes about it on the refrigerator: *pumpkin committee meeting, Wednesday, 10:30* and *call Mr. Brown about pumpkins.*

Still, I wanted to make sure. "How's the pumpkin committee going?" I asked Mother. "Is it a lot of work?"

"Well, it's a lot of time asking people to donate pumpkins and a lot of time lugging pumpkins around," she said, "but I don't mind."

"Because you'd rather collect pumpkins," I said, "instead of being, oh, some witch or Mrs. Ghost or something?"

"No," she said, "because I just want this to be the best Halloween ever!"

My mother was going to be very disappointed, I thought. Now that the Herdmans weren't coming for sure, the Woodrow Wilson Halloween looked a *little* better, but not much, and not to everybody.

Charlie wasn't the only one who checked out the supermarket and the empty shelves—there were kids there every afternoon, remembering where their favorite candy always used to be.

" . . . M&M's on the top shelf at the end" . . . "Reese's Pieces right in the middle, between two kinds of Hershey's Kisses" . . . "Milk Duds on the bottom, beside Jujubes . . . "

Boomer remembered the year there weren't any raisin-and-nut Chunkies. "They were my favorite," he said, "and I had to collect something else."

Louella missed Peanut Butter Cups and I missed Starbursts, but what we all really missed was just Halloween candy on Halloween.

The only good thing about it was that it would be Herdman-free, which, according to Alice, was the whole idea in the first place.

"We were wrong about the homework," she reported. "That wasn't why Mr. Crabtree decided to have Halloween at school. The mayor made him have Halloween at school so they could keep track of the Herdmans, my mother said."

"But they aren't coming," I said.

"Well, the mayor didn't know that would happen, and Mr. Crabtree didn't know that would happen, but at least *we* get to have a Herdman-free Halloween!"

Alice was so pleased with herself and her inside information that she didn't even notice who was standing around to *hear* the inside information, but I did.

Besides me and Louella, there was Boomer Malone and Gloria Coburn and Junior Jacobs. And, right outside the door, taking in every word and repeating "Herdman-free?" to herself . . . was Imogene.

6

"Now exactly how did she look?" Louella asked me. "Did she look mad? What do you think they'll do? Do you think they'll come after all?" She was pacing up and down the hall, really nervous. "I think they will, just to *show* the mayor and Mr. Crabtree and Alice's mother."

Of course Louella was worried about whether to tell her mother, " . . . because if I do bring Howard and then the Herdmans show up anyway, I'll get killed, plus I won't get my eight dollars!"

I thought she was probably right about the eight dollars. The last time the Herdmans got their hands on Howard, Imogene and Leroy drew pictures all over his bald head and charged people twenty-five cents to look at him. Howard didn't seem to mind, but Mrs. McCluskey had a fit. "Who knows what they'd do to him next," she said, "if they ever got the chance?"

Louella would have to make up her mind in a hurry, though, because Halloween was only two days away. This was all Charlie knew how to say lately. "It's only four days away . . . three days away . . . ," and now, "It's only two days away, Beth. When are you going to help us with our costume?"

Charlie had changed his mind about being a Happy Hobo, and he and Cecil Farmer were going to be the front and back of a lion. "We always wanted to be a two-person thing," Cecil told me, "but it wouldn't ever work with trick-or-treating. So this is our chance."

They used Mrs. Farmer's E-Z Wring floor mop to be the lion's mane—Charlie put it on his head with all the strings hanging down for me to see—and the rest of the lion would be Charlie and Cecil underneath the old slipcover.

I had to pin it around them. "Cut some eyeholes for Cecil to see out of," Charlie said.

It didn't look much like a lion, and cutting eyeholes for Cecil wouldn't help, but of course he didn't want to walk around all night and see nothing but the inside of a slipcover. I only had time to cut one hole because Cecil had to get back home with the mop, but he would have more time, he said, on Halloween night.

He also said he wouldn't do this at all if the Herdmans were going to be there. "I wouldn't even be the front half of the lion if the Herdmans were there."

I didn't blame him, but front or back, it wouldn't matter. If the Herdmans decided to take the lion apart, neither end would be safe.

Boomer Malone offered to be half of the lion if Cecil changed his mind. "I was going to be King Kong after all," Boomer said, "but my grandmother sent her fur coat to the cleaners in case it had bugs, and it got stolen." He sighed. "I even bought a gorilla mask."

"Then you can still be King Kong," I said. "You could wear a sweatshirt or something."

Boomer shook his head. "Not without my grandmother's coat."

I could understand that. In the fur coat and the gorilla mask Boomer would be a terrific King Kong, but without it he would just be a fake ape in a sweatshirt. Not too good.

Of course he might be the *only* fake ape in a sweatshirt. So far I had heard about kids who were going to be rock stars, and kids who were going to be aliens, and some super-heroes, and a human fly, but no apes.

Joanne McCoy was going to be Imogene Herdman. "Why not?" Joanne said. "They aren't going to be there."

Charlie said the same thing when I told him about Boomer's offer to be half of the lion if Cecil changed his mind.

"Why would Cecil change his mind?" Charlie asked.

"You know what he said . . . if the Herdmans come to school on Halloween he doesn't want to be inside a slipcover."

"But they aren't coming," Charlie said. "They all said so. They won't be there. Everybody knows that."

Mrs. Hazelwood wanted to make sure. "I certainly hope we're going to see you in costume, Imogene," she said on Halloween morning. This was a big lie—Mrs. Hazelwood didn't want to see Imogene at all—so she probably had her fingers crossed behind her back.

"We can't come," Imogene said. "Our mother won't let us."

Imogene would have to cross her fingers and her feet and her toes and her tonsils to cover *that* lie. Her mother probably didn't even know there *was* a Woodrow Wilson Halloween party.

If Mrs. Herdman didn't hang around the house much, she didn't hang around the school at all . . . and she probably thought PTA stood for Put Trash Away, like the signs on the trash barrels all over town.

Mrs. Hazelwood looked relieved anyway, and she didn't even bother to say "Oh, that's too bad," which would have been the normal teacher thing to say if it was anybody but a Herdman.

"Oh, honestly!" Alice muttered. "Their

mother won't let them! What place could be safer than Woodrow Wilson School tonight?"

Imogene—nose-to-nose with Alice—gave her a long, steady, squinchy-eyed Herdman look. "Any place will be safer than Woodrow Wilson School tonight," she said, and then, poking Alice in the stomach with each word, "any . . . other . . . place."

Alice gulped and turned pale—and cross-eyed, from having Imogene right in her face—but she managed to squeak out that the PTA and Mr. Crabtree and her mother would all make sure that everything would be perfectly safe. "You'll see!" she said.

"No," Imogene said . . . poke . . . poke . . . "*you'll* see."

Well. News about this spread from class to class in the halls and the lunchroom, and by the end of the day it was all anybody could talk about.

Did Imogene know something mysterious

that no one else knew? Did all the Herdmans know it, and was that the real reason they were going to stay away? And what did they know?

And, most of all, what was going to happen, tonight, at Woodrow Wilson School?

7

When I got home Charlie was already there, which was surprising, and he was all upset, which wasn't surprising.

"Something's going to happen tonight!" he said.

"Well," I said, "Halloween's going to happen, just like it always does on October thirty-first."

"But the Herdmans—," he began.

"They aren't even going to be there," I reminded him, "so what could they do?"

Actually they could do a lot. History was full of things that happened after they left— kids in the revolving door; their cat in a washing machine at the Laundromat; half-drowned turkeys at the turkey farm.

I didn't know what they could do at Woodrow Wilson School on Halloween night, but I did know that they were Herdmans, after all, and I had seen Imogene's face outside the door and heard her saying, "Herdman-free?"

Still, I knew Charlie really wanted to go to the Halloween party and be half of a lion in peace. Besides, how did I know what would happen . . . or might happen?

So I said, "Don't worry about it," and he looked relieved.

He was home early, he said, because " . . . Miss Seaworthy let us out early, but we're not supposed to tell anyone. She had us leave two or three at a time, down the stairs, past the boiler room, and out the back door."

I had never heard of one teacher, all by herself, letting her class leave early. "Why did she do that?"

"She has to get ready to be the swamp witch, she said. Besides, our room is going to be the swamp, and that takes time."

"Even so, I don't think she's allowed to do that."

Charlie nodded. "I know. That's probably why we weren't supposed to tell anybody. But I think there was someone in the boiler room. I think someone saw us leave, so will Miss Seaworthy get in trouble?"

I didn't think so. Everybody had already said that the whole school should get out early so the PTA could move in and set things up.

"All those children will be in the way!" Mrs. Wendleken had complained.

"No," my mother said. "*We'll* be in the way. After all, this Halloween party is for them."

But it wasn't, really. It was for the mayor and Mr. Crabtree and the fire chief and the police chief and all the storekeepers like Mr. Kline—everybody who wanted the Herdmans off the streets on Halloween.

There was a note from Mother on the refrigerator. *Gone to school with pumpkins,* it said. *If I don't get back in time you and Charlie can come with Louella. Mrs. Coburn broke her ankle and can't be a witch, so . . .* Here the paper had got caught in the refrigerator door and torn off, so we didn't know what the rest of it said.

"She won't be here?" Charlie said. "She won't see our lion!"

"She'll see you at school," I said.

"But she's always here when we get our costumes on and go out for trick-or-treating!"

"This year is different," I said.

"I'll say," he grumbled.

I didn't know whether Charlie was missing

Mother or missing trick-or-treating or missing the candy or just generally missing a normal Halloween, but he did cheer up when Cecil arrived with the E-Z Wring floor mop, dripping.

"Cecil," I said, "it's all wet!"

"It was a lot wetter before," he said. "My mother forgot and washed the kitchen floor. I put the mop in the clothes dryer and that helped some, but it began to smell funny."

It still smelled funny, so I thought Cecil might offer to be the front half of the lion and wear the wet mop, but he didn't offer and Charlie didn't ask, so I went ahead and pinned them into the slipcover.

I had to cut extra eyeholes for Cecil so he could see out in every direction, but Charlie could hardly see out at all because the wet mop strings were all stuck together.

"It's like being in a car at the car wash," he said, "when those long rubbery things slap up over the windshield and you can't see anything."

"You don't have to see anything for a while," I told him. "You can hang on to Louella or me till we get to school, and by then the mop will probably dry out and we can get the strings out of your face."

"And then I'll be able to see, right?" he said. "In case something happens, right?"

Cecil had the same thought. "If something happens," he said, "and I have to get out of the slipcover in a hurry, can I just leave it there?"

Louella, too. "It isn't fair," she said. "Either we have to worry because the Herdmans are going to be there messing everything up, or we have to worry because the Herdmans *aren't* going to be there, so whatever is going to happen tonight won't happen to them. It'll happen to us."

As usual, Louella was a Pilgrim, " . . . but

my mother had to pin my skirt together," she said, "so I look like a fat Pilgrim, and I don't think there were any fat Pilgrims, except maybe on Thanksgiving Day, with the big dinner and all."

"Look at me," I said. "Do you know of any belly dancers who wear sneakers?" My mother had said I absolutely could not wear flip-flops with sequins glued all over them. "Not in October," she said.

"I don't know any belly dancers at all," Louella said, "and I don't know anyone who does. But everybody *knows* what Pilgrims look like."

Actually I was glad to have sneakers on because not only did we have to keep Charlie and Cecil together and headed in the right direction but we also had to push Howard in his stroller.

Howard was in costume, too, but Louella had to tell me what it was. "He's a Chia Pet," she said. "One of those things that grow grass when you water their heads."

Once you knew that was what Howard was supposed to be, you could see that it was perfect for him because his hair—now that he had some—grew right straight up in the air.

"Of course you have to pretend his head is green all over," Louella said. "My mother would kill me if it *was* green."

"Lucky for you the Herdmans aren't here," I said. "They'd fix that."

"O-o-o-h!" Louella stopped. "What if they are here? I mean, not at school, but here. . . . " She pointed to the house at the corner of our street, where there were two big trees and a hedge of bushes. "There, maybe . . . "

Naturally when Louella stopped, I stopped and Charlie stopped, but Cecil didn't. He ran into Charlie, and they both stumbled around inside the slipcover until we stood them up and straightened them out.

"Remember I can't see very much," Cecil said, "so if you stop you have to tell me. You have to say 'Stop!'"

We had to say "Stop!" a lot, till even Howard began to fuss about being jolted up and down in his stroller.

"I'm sorry," Louella said, "but I feel like I can see Herdmans everywhere."

I didn't see Herdmans, but I didn't really blame Louella for feeling spooky. It was almost dark now so the streetlights were on, making pools of light here and there. There was enough wind to make the dry leaves fall and rustle underfoot, and there were other kids—just shapes of bats and ghosts and outer-space bugs in the shadowy night.

It really felt like Halloween, until . . .

"I see a big light!" Cecil said—pleased, I guess, that he could finally see something out of his eyeholes.

The "big light" was Woodrow Wilson School. It was lit up from top to bottom, all bright and cheerful, as if to scare Halloween away and leave a perfectly safe school event—free of shrieking ghosts and rattling skeletons, free of all Halloween tricks and all Halloween candy.

And free of all Herdmans . . .

8

This was a new experience—being Herdman-free on Halloween—and you could tell not everyone believed it. Louella, for instance, kept looking over her shoulder for anybody who looked unusual.

"Louella," I said, "*Everybody* looks unusual. It's Halloween."

Charlie and Cecil looked unusual as long as they stayed together, and even more unusual when they didn't. Kenneth Jordan was a robot in aluminum foil, with Slinkies for ears and an alarm clock taped to the front of him. There were two or three television sets—Joyce Bender, with a box over her head and a red wig, was pretending to be *I Love Lucy*. Skinny Austin Hubbard was a floor lamp in brown wrapping paper, with a lamp shade on his head and a flashlight to turn himself on. Maxine Cooper was a big round yellow M&M—the only candy in sight.

"I know," Louella said, "but I keep thinking I'll see some Herdmans after all, and they'll grab Howard and shave off what little hair he's got."

"You will see Imogene," I told her, "but it won't really be Imogene. It'll be Joanne McCoy."

But Joanne changed her mind and came in a Wonder Woman costume " . . . because," she said, "if something *does* happen, and people think I'm Imogene Herdman, they'll blame it on me."

It was hard to imagine what could happen here that hadn't been planned out and arranged by the PTA and Mrs. Wendleken. The whole place looked like Back-to-School-Night.

On Back-to-School Night there are signs on all the doors so the parents won't get lost, the PA system is on with Mr. Crabtree giving directions and advice, and there are special exhibits in the halls—science projects and shoe-box dioramas and, once, Alice's popcorn map of Antarctica, which was pretty impressive till Claude and Ollie Herdman ate it, glue and all.

Now, on Halloween night, it was almost the same.

There were signs on all the doors: "Ghoul Gallery," "Mystery Swamp," "Ghostly Games." The PA system was on with lots of screeches and ghoulish laughter. "That's Jolene Liggett's father on the PA," Louella said, "but don't tell her I told you. She's too embarrassed."

There were exhibits, too—stacks of my mother's pumpkins everywhere, cardboard bats hanging from the ceiling, and a big scarecrow right inside the front door.

"That's Dad's wash-the-car pants on the scarecrow," Charlie said.

He was right, and this was good news for two reasons: it meant Charlie could see around the mop strings and I wouldn't have to lead him everywhere; and it meant my father probably wouldn't get drafted at the last minute to be the swamp zombie or something since he already gave them his pants.

Of course nobody wore costumes on Back-to-School Night, so that was different. Now there were all the usual cartoon characters and ghosts and accident victims, some strange Dracula-types all wrapped up in black . . . and a King Kong. We saw Boomer at the end of the hall, all brown and furry, in a gorilla mask, so they must have found his grandmother's coat.

Alice got her wish—she was the only Christmas tree. She had lights and decorations hung all over herself, with a big star on top of her head and jingle bells glued to her shoes. There was a long extension cord, too, hanging down her back, so you knew that sooner or later she would plug herself in somewhere and light herself up.

"Howard will like that," Louella said, "and it won't be too scary for him."

We weren't supposed to take Howard to anything scary, but so far that didn't look like much of a problem. We even heard Mr. Crabtree tell two kindergarten mothers, "Don't you worry, there's nothing scary here!"

I guess that was important to the kindergarten mothers, but who knows what's scary to kindergarten kids? Eloise Albright's little brother is scared of fish; Wesley Potter's little sister is scared of bald people, so she was probably scared of Howard till something sprouted on his head. Charlie used to be scared of Little Orphan Annie in old comic books because she didn't have any eyes—just round white circles.

So we really couldn't know what would be scary to Howard . . . but almost the first thing we saw was scary to me.

It was my mother, in a crooked witch hat and her take-out-the-trash sneakers, swooping back and forth in front of the Mystery Maze.

"Now, Beth . . . " She swooped—sort of—over to me. "Don't look at me that way. I told you abut this, that Mrs. Coburn broke her ankle, and . . . "

Then I remembered the torn-off note on the refrigerator. This was what it said—that my mother was going to be a witch for everyone to see.

"After all," Mother went on, "it's not as if I *want* to be doing this, and I'm certainly no good at it, but somebody had to fill in for Thelma Coburn. So, are you having a good time?" She turned to Louella. "How about Howard . . . is he having a good time?"

"I guess so, Mrs. Bradley," Louella said. "He's not scared, anyway."

"Oh, no," Mother said, swooping back to the Mystery Maze, "there's nothing scary here!"

"That must be the whole idea," Louella said, "but I thought the whole idea was no Herdmans."

"Maybe it's the same thing," I said.

With nothing scary, nothing spooky, nothing unexpected, no trick or treat and no candy, and not even Herdmans to watch out for, it was turning into the worst Halloween ever.

This is what everybody said—Boomer,

Stewart, Joanne, Rosalie Sims, Albert Pelfrey—" . . . worst Halloween ever . . . " Even Alice was grumpy because she couldn't find a convenient outlet to plug herself in.

"I remember last year," Maxine Cooper said with a sigh. "Remember the house where they strung cobwebs everywhere, and the door was creaky, and the doorbell was one awful scream?"

"And the house where they gave out the big candy bars?" somebody said.

"I got fifty-seven different things last year," Albert said, "and they were all good . . . chocolate and peanut butter and . . ."

"How do you know that?" Alice barked at him. "Did Ralph Herdman tell you you had fifty-seven different things after he took your sack?"

Alice was especially grumpy with Albert because she could tell that, next to her, he had the best costume of all, and it didn't depend on electricity. Albert had half a laundry basket tied to the front of him, with clothes hanging out of it, and bottles of detergent and bleach stuck in among the clothes. A sign across his back said "Dirty Laundry."

"But it's not really dirty," Albert said. "It's just old stuff, full of holes."

"Too bad I didn't know, Albert," I said. "My whole family is here in old stuff full of holes. My brother's in an old slipcover; I'm in old bedroom curtains; my mother's wearing her take-out-the-trash sneakers; and my father's wash-the-car pants are on the scarecrow."

"Is he in them?" Stewart asked. "Your father?"

"No, it's just his pants. He isn't in them."

"Well"—Stewart shrugged—"someone is."

He was right. There was somebody inside the scarecrow costume . . . reaching up to scratch its head, crossing one leg over the other one. . . .

"I don't think it's your father," Louella said. "It's not tall enough, and it's *too* tall to be your brother."

"It doesn't have to be someone from my family, Louella, just because it's our pants," I said.

"It's probably just some short teacher," Boomer said.

He was right behind us, and I suddenly remembered seeing Boomer twice before. Once he was King Kong, and once he was . . . I turned around.

Boomer was a Happy Hobo.

"Boomer!" I said. "Where's your costume?"

"This is it. Remember, I told you."

"But you were King Kong!" That was Louella. "We saw you."

"I saw you, too," Joanne said, "in some old fur coat."

"My grandmother's coat!" Boomer said. "Who's in my grandmother's coat?"

Who was in my father's pants? I wondered.

Who was the scarecrow? Who was King Kong?

"**A**ttention, please!"

Everybody jumped, but it was only Mr. Crabtree on the PA system.

"Will the following boys and girls join your parents in front of the office on the first floor: Missy Reed, Joey Marks, Eliot and Andrew Baker, Jillian Anthony, Freddy Adams. Thank you."

There were the usual crackles on the PA system, and then we could hear the school secretary whispering, " . . . and there's more.

Wanda Ruggles and the Quincy boy, and Mrs. Walker can't find Robert, and the Lenkers can't find Gretchen. . . . "

It sounded as if most of the first grade was missing somewhere in Woodrow Wilson School, and if this was true it was the only interesting thing that had happened all evening.

" . . . not just the younger kids," the secretary was saying, "Eddie O'Brien, too, and Danny Filus, and Junior Jacobs . . . "

Danny? Junior? They were in our class.

There were more crackles, and little bits of what other people were saying—the secretary, Mr. Crabtree, parents—" . . . left him at the Mystery Swamp . . . saw him with some ghost . . . brought her little sister and now she can't find her . . ."

At this, Louella grabbed Howard out of his stroller as if she thought he might just suddenly decide to get up and follow the crowd.

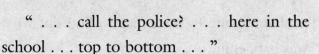

" . . . call the police? . . . here in the school . . . top to bottom . . . "

There was a loud *clunk* . . . and no more news on the PA system.

We all looked at one another, and everyone was thinking the same thing—Was this it? The Curse of the Herdmans?

"Any place will be safer," Imogene had said, "than Woodrow Wilson School tonight."

I looked around for Alice, to see if she remembered anything else about that conversation. Had Imogene said something that I didn't hear, like, "Don't bother to do your homework. You won't need it after tonight"?

But Alice had left, still looking for an outlet, and we could hear all her ornaments, clicking and clacking as she went down the hall.

The scarecrow was gone, too, but he (or she, depending on which teacher it was) had

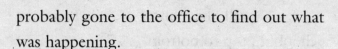

probably gone to the office to find out what was happening.

"I knew it!" Joanne squeaked. "I knew this would happen. And somehow *they* knew it would happen, and that's why they're not here. You know what Imogene said."

Everyone knew what Imogene said: "Any place will be safer."

"And the PA system isn't working, so we don't know who else is missing," Joanne went on, "so you better hang on to your little brother, Louella."

Louella didn't need to be told that. She was holding Howard so tight around his middle that he was all folded over. If he'd had anything to say about it, he would probably rather be missing than be halfway upside down.

It was Joanne's idea for us all to stay together—so if we disappeared, I guess, we'd have company our own age instead of all the first-graders.

And, naturally, it was Albert's idea for us to hang out near the cider and dough-nuts " . . . before they're all gone," he said. "Remember the spring concert!"

All those refreshments disappeared after Leroy Herdman set off the fire alarm in the middle of Alice Wendleken's piano solo. Of course everybody had to vacate the building, and of course there wasn't any fire, and of course there weren't any refreshments left when everybody got back. No more piano solo either, though, which was good news for everyone except Alice and her mother.

It wasn't unusual for food to disappear when the Herdmans were around, but it would be unusual, now, for seventeen dozen doughnuts to disappear when they *weren't* around, so I didn't think Albert had anything to worry about.

I didn't think I had anything to worry about either, till Howard's stroller got caught on something and the something turned out to be my mother's slipcover, with all its safety pins and eyeholes.

I remembered what Cecil had said: "If something happens and I have to get out of the slipcover in a hurry, can I just leave it there?"

I must have said yes, because here it was.

"You must have said yes," Louella echoed.

"But why would they get out of their costume?" I couldn't understand this because they wanted to be in the costume parade and maybe win the prize. "I was even supposed to find them and be sure they were still all pinned together."

"Maybe they saw Albert in his laundry basket," Louella said, "and figured he would win the costume prize. Maybe they just got discouraged. Or maybe, like Cecil said, something happened." And then she added, "To them."

Normally I would have said, "Come on, Louella. What's going to happen to my brother that hasn't already happened to him? He's been painted green, wallpapered, stuck in a revolving door." Normally I would have figured that Charlie just fell out of his costume somehow.

But I didn't have a chance to say anything because at that very minute all the lights went out, leaving Woodrow Wilson School as black as the Halloween night outside.

10

At any other time it wouldn't matter if the lights went out at Woodrow Wilson School. For one thing, we probably wouldn't be there if it happened at night . . . and when it *had* happened, once, in the daytime, Mrs. Hazelwood turned it into a lesson about energy sources and we had to draw wiring diagrams for extra credit.

But now . . . on Halloween night . . .

"I knew this would happen!" Joanne said, again, but of course she didn't know this would happen. She didn't even know *what* had happened.

Nobody knew what had happened, except Donald Sycamore, because Donald was the only person around when Alice finally found an outlet and plugged herself in.

Donald said later that it was very exciting, " . . . just like the Fourth of July. There was this loud crack and a lot of sparks and Alice yelled and the lights went out."

Alice wasn't hurt, but for a long time she claimed to have loose electricity in her fingers, and she wouldn't turn anything on or plug anything in because of it.

In the meantime, though, everyone was stumbling around in the dark.

Normally when something unexpected happened, Mr. Crabtree would get on the PA system and tell us all about it: the big red stain on the lunchroom floor was catsup, not blood; the kindergarten slide was missing from the playground, and the kindergarten kids were not allowed to use the big slide; today's scheduled fire drill would be postponed till next Tuesday.

"What do you think he'll tell us about this?" Joanne's voice came out of the darkness.

"Probably tell us the lights are out," Stewart said.

"No, he won't." Boomer sounded funny. "He can't tell us anything. Remember? The PA system's broken."

"Then what's that?" Louella said, after a second.

I had heard it, too—a low, drawn-out whistle, like wind through a loose window . . . but there was no wind here, and no loose window.

"I can't see anything!" Joanne said. "I don't even know where we are!"

"I don't even know *who* we are," Louella whispered to me, "because, listen . . . Howard's stroller is gone. It was right here, and now it's gone. Who took Howard's stroller?" She raised her voice. "Who took Howard's stroller?"

"Not me-e-e," someone said, just like that: "me-e-e."

"Don't fool around, Boomer," Louella said. "I have to find Howard's stroller."

"I'm not fooling around," Boomer said. "I don't know who that was. It wasn't me."

It also wasn't Albert or Stewart or Joanne or Maxine or me, so we didn't hang around there—wherever "there" was. Joanne was right. Everything seemed different with all the lights out and no way to tell one room from another.

"But who *was* it?" Louella said as we picked our way down the dark hall, bumping into what we hoped was each other, "and where *is* Howard's stroller?"

I didn't know who "it" was, but I did know that we'd better find Howard's stroller in a hurry, or I would have to help Louella carry him, and Howard was a lump.

We headed for voices, because we weren't the only people temporarily lost in Woodrow Wilson School. Everywhere there were kids and parents hollering for other kids and parents—"Jolene! . . . Gloria! . . . Wayne, where are you? . . . Boyd Liggett, you come here to me by the office!"— and Mr. Crabtree was yelling, "Lights! Lights!" as if just yelling about them would turn them on somehow.

We did see a little flicker of light, way at the end of the hall. "Like a flashlight!" Boomer said. "Austin Hubbard had a flashlight because he's a floor lamp. Hey Austin!" he called. "Wait up!"

But the light bobbed up and down and back and forth, and then went out.

Maybe Austin didn't hear us, I thought. Or maybe it wasn't Austin. Maybe it was . . . Who? or What?

Something brushed against my head—
one of the cardboard bats?—and then Louella
squealed, "O-o-o-h! There goes Howard!"

Of course he didn't go far, and he didn't
seem to mind being dropped on the floor,
but I had to feel around a little bit so I
wouldn't pick him up by one leg or something . . . and by accident I grabbed Joanne,
who also squealed.

"It's me!" I said. "It's just me."

"How am I supposed to know that?" she
groaned. "You could be anybody . . . or anything. I'm going to sit down on the floor and
stay right here till the lights come on. But
somebody has to stay with me."

I had the perfect person—Howard—but
before I could hand him off to Joanne, we
heard somebody yelling, above all the other
noise.

"It's alive! The whole cauldron is alive
with worms!" The somebody was my mother.

11

When we got to her, Mother had calmed down. By now some people had flash-lights so I could see that her witch hat was bent in the middle and hanging down over her face. She looked a little cross-eyed, especially up close when she hugged me.

"It isn't worms," she said. "At least, it isn't all worms. I think it's *some* worms and a lot of cold spaghetti. I don't know how it all got into the boiling cauldron. . . . Boiling cauldron, hah! Boiling with squirmy worms!

Anyway," she went on, "I only left for a minute, to see if I could find you and Charlie, and when I came back . . . ughgh!"

"I thought you were in charge of the Mystery Maze," I said.

"Not after some cat showed up and all but tore the whole thing down—scratching and squalling and leaving its fur everywhere . . . and not even its own fur. Somebody had painted it black, for Halloween, I guess."

She leaned closer. "Goodness, I wish they would get the lights back on. I can't quite see who's with you."

"Well," I said, "Howard's with me, and Louella, Boomer, and Maxine . . . "

"Not Charlie?" Mother said. "Or Cecil? Have you seen them . . . him . . . it?"

She was pretty upset, so I just said yes, which wasn't really a lie, because I had seen "it"—the lion costume.

Then Mother said I should go get them,

since I knew where they were.

"They may not still be there," I said.

"Oh, they won't go roaming around in the dark," she said, "especially not in a slip-cover and a floor mop."

"You don't know where they are," Louella said as we left.

This was true, but I knew where the slipcover and floor mop were—in the downstairs hall by the teachers' room, which is where we all went, leaving my mother to deal with her wormy spaghetti.

By now our eyes had begun to adjust to the darkness, but . . . "Even so," Joanne said, "everything is too spooky."

The hall to the teachers' room was more than spooky. It was deserted.

"That's because there's nothing special set up here," Stewart said. "No Haunted Hall or Monster's Mansion . . . just the teachers' room. I've never been in the teachers' room," he added. "What do they keep in there?"

"Kids," I said, "according to Imogene Herdman."

That was what Imogene told Charlie— that if kids went in the teachers' room they never got out again. "The teachers keep them in there," Imogene said, "with little bowls of water and old bologna sandwiches."

"Come on," Stewart said. "What do they do in there?"

"Ask Leroy," Louella said. "According to him they hang out, watch TV, drink beer, order in pizza. I don't know what they do. I've never been in there."

"Me, either," Albert said. "I never got invited."

"Albert," I said, "nobody gets invited to the teachers' room. Sometimes you get sent there with a note for someone, but even then they don't let you in."

"I got sent there once in the second grade,"

Maxine said, "with a note for Mrs. Campbell. I didn't even know who Mrs. Campbell was, and I was so nervous I got a nosebleed." She stopped at the door. "I'm not even sure I want to go in there now."

I didn't know whether Maxine was scared—in case Imogene was right and there was something in the teachers' room to be scared *of*—or whether she was just remembering her nosebleed and wondering if it would always happen when she went to the teachers' room.

"There's just tables and chairs," Boomer reported from inside the room. "No TV or anything good. But there's somebody in here-re. . . . " His voice faded out, or down, or away.

"Sounds like he fell in a hole," Louella said.

Then I remembered what Alice had told me about the teachers' room. "I think he did," I said.

As usual, Alice was right. There *was* a hole in the floor, and Boomer was at the bottom of the hole, along with " . . . Danny and Junior and a lot of first-grade kids, and Charlie's here. . . . "

"We're in the boiler room," Cecil chimed in, "but we took off our costume before we slid down, and left it . . . "

Slid down?

Suddenly the lights came on again and we could see the hole and, inside it, the missing kindergarten slide, and down at the bottom . . .

"What's down there?" Albert said. "It looks like—"

"Candy!" Charlie whooped. "Halloween candy! The whole boiler room is full of Halloween candy. I th-th-think it's . . . I think it's . . . " He was so excited, he was stuttering. "I think it's all the candy in the world!"

12

That's what it looked like—wall-to-wall candy, big piles of candy, the floor covered with candy, all kinds, all colors, all wrapped—a giant trick-or-treat supply for the rest of your life.

Milk Duds, Sugar Babies, PEZ, Milky Way, Snickers, DumDums, 3 Musketeers, Hershey's bars, Swedish Fish, Jujubes, KitKats, Twizzlers, Crunch bars, Twix, Tootsie Rolls, Mounds bars, Starbursts, Smartees, Reese's Pieces, M&M's, Reese's Peanut Butter Cups, PayDay bars, Almond Joy, Baby Ruth, 5th Avenue,

Mr. Goodbar, Rolos, Butterfingers, Caramello, Candy Dots, Hershey's Kisses, Skor bars, licorice whips, Heath bars, Raisinets, Mallo Cups, Charleston Chew, Chunkies, Clark bars, Krackel, Whoppers, Sugar Daddies, Oh Henry!, Bit-O-Honey, DoveBar, Goobers, Sno-Caps, Junior mints.

We had all come down the kindergarten slide—even Albert in his laundry basket and Louella holding Howard—so it was pretty crowded in the boiler room with all of us and all the missing kids.

Anybody who had pockets in their costume was stuffing them with candy and anybody who didn't was welcome, Albert said, to borrow part of his laundry basket.

"That's really nice of you, Albert," I said. "You don't have to do that."

"Yes, I do," he said. "If I took all the candy for myself, I'd have to go to fat camp again this summer."

"I wish I had Howard's stroller," Louella said. "It has a big pocket at the back and we could fill it up." She sighed. "I guess Pilgrims didn't have pockets."

"Neither do belly dancers," I said, but I didn't really care. It was almost enough just to *be* there in a sea of candy.

Of course you had to wonder where it all came from, but it was a lot easier to figure out where it *didn't* come from, which would be the PTA or Mr. Crabtree or the mayor or— this was Charlie's idea—some kind of Halloween tooth fairy.

I guess that sounded good to the first-graders, because when Mr. Crabtree showed up and yelled, *"Where did all this come from?"* Missy Reed told him that it came from the Halloween tooth fairy.

It's a good thing Missy was a first-grader, and cute, because Mr. Crabtree's ears turned red at the top the way they had when Ollie

Herdman wrote the dirty words on Rhoda Gallagher's turtle.

This was a lot worse than that, though, and Mr. Crabtree's ears were a lot redder. After all, Rhoda could just pick up her turtle and get it out of sight and then Mr. Crabtree could pretend that there wasn't even any turtle in the first place with or without dirty words . . . but here were a lot of missing kids, and the missing kindergarten slide, and a room full of candy that had to be missing from somewhere, and Mr. Crabtree didn't know how to explain it or who to blame.

Of course neither did anyone else. "Who to blame" had never been a problem at Woodrow Wilson School—when something happened you just looked around for a Herdman. But on Halloween night at Woodrow Wilson School there weren't any Herdmans around.

Mr. Crabtree *could* have blamed Alice for the blackout, but by the time Alice lit herself up there were already kids missing and the boiler room was already full of candy.

When Mr. Crabtree cancelled the rest of the Halloween party—before anything else happened, he said—the PTA committee got stuck with fourteen dozen doughnuts, so they blamed Mr. Crabtree for that . . . and Mrs. Wendleken blamed the Ohio Light and Power Company for what she called Alice's "brush with death," but nobody else got blamed for anything.

The police chief took charge of the candy in case it turned out to be stolen, but he said he couldn't haul it off to the police station, and Mr. Crabtree said he couldn't leave it in the boiler room, so it all ended up where Halloween candy is supposed to end up— with the kids.

The manager of the supermarket said he would never stock that much candy. "You stock that much candy," he said, "you'll have stale candy."

He was right, because that's what we had—stale candy. But you can still count stale candy; you can make piles of stale candy and trade for your favorite kinds; you can eat stale candy if you want to and your mother lets you and you don't have braces.

Stale isn't very important at Halloween. What's important at Halloween is amount— how many, how much—and we had more candy that Halloween than ever before . . . or ever again, probably.

Never again at Woodrow Wilson School, for sure. That's what Mr. Crabtree said when the PTA committee wanted to store all the cardboard bats and fake cobwebs and witch hats and ghost sheets for next year.

"No next year!" he said. "Never again!"

This meant that we could go back to Halloween as usual, which was what we all really wanted in the first place.

"Why?" my mother said. "Why do you want to run all over the neighborhood in the dark, and try to keep your costume together, and hang on to your trick-or-treat sack and your flashlight, and then, on top of everything else, stay away from the Herdmans. . . . Why?"

"Yes," Charlie said, after a second.

"Yes, what?" Mother said.

"All that . . . even the Herdmans." He shrugged. "That's what Halloween is supposed to be."

Good for you, Charlie, I thought, to know that. After all, once you go down a slide into a room full of candy you might forget what an ordinary Halloween is like.

My father was still trying to get it all straight. "You went down a slide into the boiler room?" he said. "How did you happen to do that?"

"We just followed Boomer," Charlie said.

"In his gorilla suit," Cecil added.

Only I knew it wasn't Boomer.

13

There were several clues like that, but I guess Mr. Crabtree never could tie them all together, although he kept calling people into the office to ask what they saw or heard on Halloween night. He mostly asked the wrong people, though—teachers and PTA mothers and a bunch of random kids who honestly couldn't tell him anything he didn't already know.

"Just all the lights went out and you didn't know where you were and there were a lot of strange noises and spooky stuff and then a whole ton of candy!" Some of those kids also said, "Great Halloween!"

Mrs. Wendleken had a lot to say, but it was all about Alice's beautiful, but ruined, costume that never got to win a prize, and about the leftover doughnuts that were donated to the Welfare Department, " . . . so you know who got them!"

Everybody knew who got them, because the Herdmans showed up with doughnuts every day for a week.

Mr. Crabtree finally quit trying to figure it out and moved on to Thanksgiving— although every now and then you would see him go down to the boiler room and poke around the corners and shake his head.

Danny Filus and Stewart Walker helped the janitor, Mr. Sprague, move the kindergarten slide back to the playground, although Mr. Sprague said he could have done it by himself. "Those boys could have moved it," he said. "It wasn't so heavy."

Boomer's grandmother's fur coat turned up, along with my father's wash-the-car pants, in the lost-and-found box with all the hats and mittens and ugly scarves. Nobody knew how they got there, but everybody recognized the gorilla and the scarecrow because they'd followed one or the other to the candy.

My mother checked out Charlie's candy and divided it into okay, not-so-good, and break-your-teeth-off, and since she wasn't the only mother who did this, everybody had a lot of leftover candy.

The fourth grade even went to Mr. Crabtree and offered to glue all the candy together in one big pile and set it up in Woodrow Wilson School as a sculpture.

Mr. Crabtree said, "No, thank you"— "He didn't even look at the picture we drew of it," Charlie said—but Miss Seaworthy gave the whole fourth grade extra credit for "creative thinking."

Alice collected all her extra credit for the Halloween assignments and then announced that her oral report would be How It Feels to Be Almost Electrocuted.

At first Mrs. Hazelwood said no. "Our oral reports are intended to provide information," she said, "that we can all use. I don't think this is information we *want* to use. Choose another topic, Alice, of more general interest."

Actually, near electrocution—Alice's—was the most interesting topic anyone could think of, and maybe Mrs. Hazelwood realized that, so Alice got to give her report, which was very long and very boring. Who but Alice, you had to wonder, could make electrocution boring?

Then came the big surprise. Imogene Herdman began clapping even before Alice was through, and pounding and hammering on the kids sitting beside her to do the same.

"I couldn't help it," Louis Fraley said. "She had me by the ears, and she would have twisted them off. All she said was 'You better clap or you'll have two new holes in your head.'"

Naturally Louis clapped, along with Imogene's other neighbors, and they kept on clapping until Mrs. Hazelwood finally came to and said, "Very well. That will be enough now." I guess she couldn't believe her own eyes and ears, so that took a while.

At recess I found Imogene and her sack of doughnuts. They had to be pretty stale by then, but " . . . they'll make good rocks," she said.

"You must have really liked Alice's report," I said.

She shook her head. "Who cares if her ears sizzled and her toes turned blue?"

"That didn't happen. She never said it did."

"Would have made a better story."

"Imogene," I said, "you didn't even listen to her report! So what was all the clapping about?"

"We owe her." She aimed a doughnut at the back of the building and grinned, sly and sneaky. "She blew out the lights."

I guess the Herdmans didn't think of that, or if they did they couldn't figure out how to do it . . . and then here came Alice, the Christmas tree, to do it for them, and it was the perfect thing. Mysterious candy, missing kids, secret slide, and then, just like that— blackout!

It was the last straw for Mr. Crabtree, according to my mother. "That poor man!" she said. "The whole point of this was to have a Herdman-free Halloween, and do you know what he said? He said, 'I would rather have the Herdmans!'"

Well . . . he *did* have them. We all had

them. The Herdmans were all over Woodrow Wilson School on Halloween night—in Boomer's gorilla suit and my father's pants. They were the Dracula-types in long black coats—"ONGOING INVESTIGATION OF THEFTS AT MORGAN'S CLEANERS," the newspaper said that week. "WINTER GARMENTS STOLEN, PERHAPS BY THE NEEDY."

After all, who but the Herdmans had enough candy to fill up the boiler room, after years of taking everyone else's candy? Who but the Herdmans could run around stealing coats from the cleaners and slides from the playground? Who but the Herdmans would spray-paint their cat black, and who else's cat would survive that? Who but the Herdmans would think to *do* those things?

"But why?" Louella said, and there were several suggestions. "They did it for the doughnuts" was, of course, Alice's idea. "They had to get the candy out of the house," as if

Mrs. Herdman was a normal clean-up-that-mess mother. "They just wanted to ruin the PTA Halloween party. . . . "

"But wait a minute," Boomer said. "It was a really great Halloween, and the greatest trick or treat ever . . . so was that why they did it?"

"We could ask them," I said, but nobody jumped to do that, including me, because if the Herdmans wanted you to know what they had done they would tell you . . . and if they just wanted you to wonder about it you should just wonder about it and keep your mouth shut.

BARBARA ROBINSON

was born in Portsmouth, Ohio, and now makes her home in Berwyn, Pennsylvania. A graduate of Allegheny College, Ms. Robinson also received an honorary doctorate of letters from Allegheny.

Ms. Robinson has written several books for children, including MY BROTHER LOUIS MEASURES WORMS, THE BEST SCHOOL YEAR EVER, and THE BEST HALLOWEEN EVER.

THE BEST CHRISTMAS PAGEANT EVER is now a classic TV movie, and the play THE BEST CHRISTMAS PAGEANT EVER is produced annually in theaters, schools, and churches all over the U.S.

Ms. Robinson has two daughters, Carolyn and Marjorie, and three grandchildren, Tomas, Marcos, and Lucas. You can visit her online at http://usawrites4kids.drury.edu/authors/robinson.